ABOUT THE BANK STREET READY-TO-READ SERIES

Seventy years of educational research and innovative teaching have given the Bank Street College of Education the reputation as America's most trusted name in early childhood education.

Because no two children are exactly alike in their development, we have designed the *Bank Street Ready-to-Read* series in three levels to accommodate the individual stages of reading readiness of children ages four through eight.

○ *Level 1:* GETTING READY TO READ—read-alouds for children who are taking their first steps toward reading.

● *Level 2:* READING TOGETHER—for children who are just beginning to read by themselves but may need a little help.

○ *Level 3:* I CAN READ IT MYSELF—for children who can read independently.

Our three levels make it easy to select the books most appropriate for a child's development and enable him or her to grow with the series step by step. The *Bank Street Ready-to-Read* books also overlap and reinforce each other, further encouraging the reading process.

We feel that making reading fun and enjoyable is the single most important thing that you can do to help children become good readers. And we hope you'll be a part of Bank Street's long tradition of learning through sharing.

The Bank Street College of Education

For my father, with love
—E.L.S.

For Diana Rebecca
—J.O.

SIM CHUNG AND THE RIVER DRAGON

A Bantam Little Rooster Book/February 1993

Little Rooster is a trademark of Bantam Books,
a division of Bantam Doubleday Dell Publishing Group, Inc.

Series graphic design by Alex Jay/Studio J

Special thanks to James A. Levine, Betsy Gould,
and Diane Arico.

All rights reserved.
Copyright © 1993 by Byron Preiss Visual Publications, Inc.
Text copyright © 1993 by Bank Street College of Education.
Illustrations copyright © 1993 by June Otani
and Byron Preiss Visual Publications, Inc.

No part of this book may be reproduced or transmitted
in any form or by any means, electronic or mechanical,
including photocopying, recording, or by any information
storage and retrieval system, without permission in writing from
the publisher.
For information address: Bantam Books

Library of Congress Cataloging-in-Publication Data
Schecter, Ellen.
Sim Chung and the river dragon;
a folktale from Korea / retold by Ellen Schecter ;
illustrated by June Otani.
p.   cm. — (Bank Street ready-to-read)
"A Byron Preiss book."
"A Bantam little rooster book."
Summary: In order to obtain a cure
for her father's blindness, a loving young girl
agrees to marry a terrifying dragon.
ISBN 0-553-09117-4. — ISBN 0-553-37109-6 (pbk.)
[1. Folklore—Korea.]   I. Otani, June, ill.
II. Title.   III. Series.
PZ8.1.S317Si   1993
398.2'09519—dc20
[E]
92-7652   CIP   AC

Published simultaneously in the United States and Canada

Bantam Books are published by Bantam Books, a division of Bantam Doubleday
Dell Publishing Group, Inc. Its trademark, consisting of the words "Bantam Books"
and the portrayal of a rooster, is Registered in U.S. Patent and Trademark Office
and in other countries. Marca Registrada. Bantam Books, 666 Fifth Avenue, New
York, New York 10103.

PRINTED IN THE UNITED STATES OF AMERICA

0 9 8 7 6 5 4 3 2 1

Sim Chung
and the River Dragon

A Folktale from Korea

Retold by Ellen Schecter
Illustrated by June Otani

A Byron Preiss Book

A BANTAM LITTLE ROOSTER BOOK
NEW YORK · TORONTO · LONDON · SYDNEY · AUCKLAND

Chapter 1:
The Promise

Long ago,
in the Land of Morning Brightness,
a man and wife wished and waited
many years for a child.

Then the wife had a dream.
She floated in a garden full of
flowers and fruits and singing birds.
Suddenly, a star fell from heaven
into her heart.

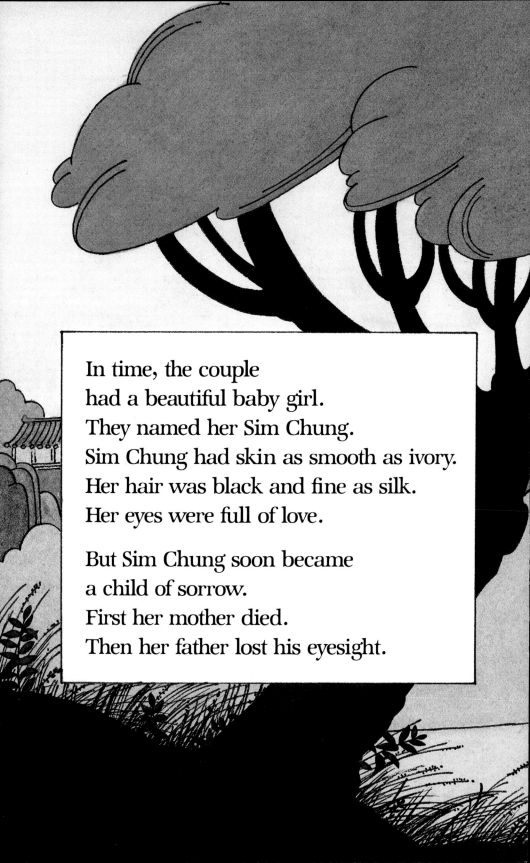

In time, the couple
had a beautiful baby girl.
They named her Sim Chung.
Sim Chung had skin as smooth as ivory.
Her hair was black and fine as silk.
Her eyes were full of love.

But Sim Chung soon became
a child of sorrow.
First her mother died.
Then her father lost his eyesight.

Year by year,
Sim Chung and her father
grew poorer and poorer.
They sold all their things,
one by one, so they could eat.

When they went out,
Sim Chung guided her father
step by step
along the crowded streets.
But Sim Chung never complained.
And she shone like a star
in her father's heart.

Then, one day, Sim Chung's father
went out alone to beg for coins.
He fell into a deep ditch
and called for help.

A strong hand pulled him out.
A strange voice spoke to him.
"Give me three hundred bags of rice,"
said the priest from the temple.
"And in time
you will get your sight back."

Overjoyed, the old man quickly promised
to send the rice.
He stumbled home
and told Sim Chung what happened.

"How can we send three hundred bags of rice?" she cried out in alarm. "We have hardly enough to fill a nutshell."

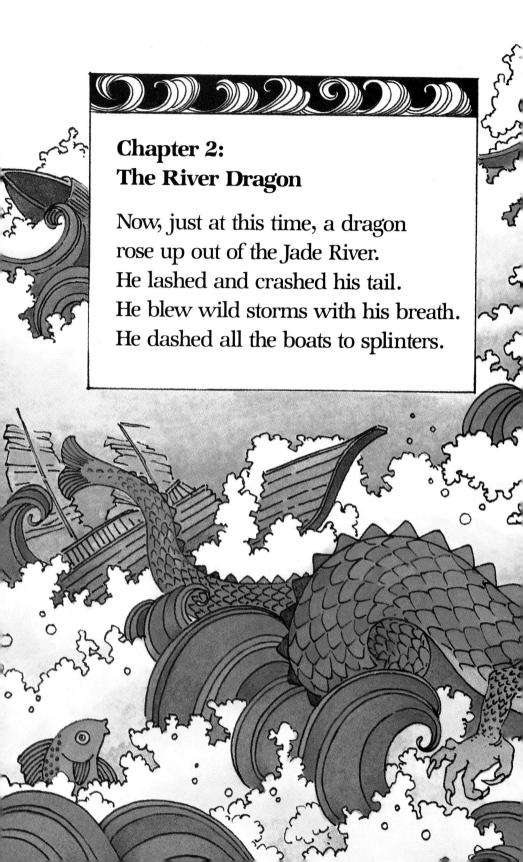

Chapter 2:
The River Dragon

Now, just at this time, a dragon
rose up out of the Jade River.
He lashed and crashed his tail.
He blew wild storms with his breath.
He dashed all the boats to splinters.

"Dragon! Stop your storms!"
begged a rich man
who owned many boats.
"No. I will not stop," roared the dragon.
"Not till a beautiful young girl comes
of her own free will to live with me."

The rich man offered a huge reward:
three hundred bags of rice.
But no girl in all Korea
would give up her life
and go to the dragon.

Then Sim Chung heard about the
river dragon and the reward.
She dressed herself
in a long white gown
and a big hat.

She slipped through the streets
and knocked at the rich man's gates
And she did all this
without one word to her father.

"I will go to the river dragon,"
she told the rich man,
"if you send three hundred bags of rice
to the temple for my father."

What a brave and beautiful girl,
the rich man thought.
Any man would be happy
with her by his side.

The rich man's heart filled with pity.
"I will send the rice,"
he promised Sim Chung.
"I give you my word."

The next morning at dawn
a long line of horses set out
from the rich man's house.
They carried three hundred bags of rice
through the morning brightness
to the temple.

Sim Chung's heart was peaceful
as she watched.
Her hands hardly shook.

But the servants wept as they
helped Sim Chung dress.
She wore a wedding gown
of deep, shining green.
She put on a headdress
glowing with gems and bright ribbons.
Jewels sparkled on her neck
like diamond drops of water.
Now she was ready to meet the dragon.

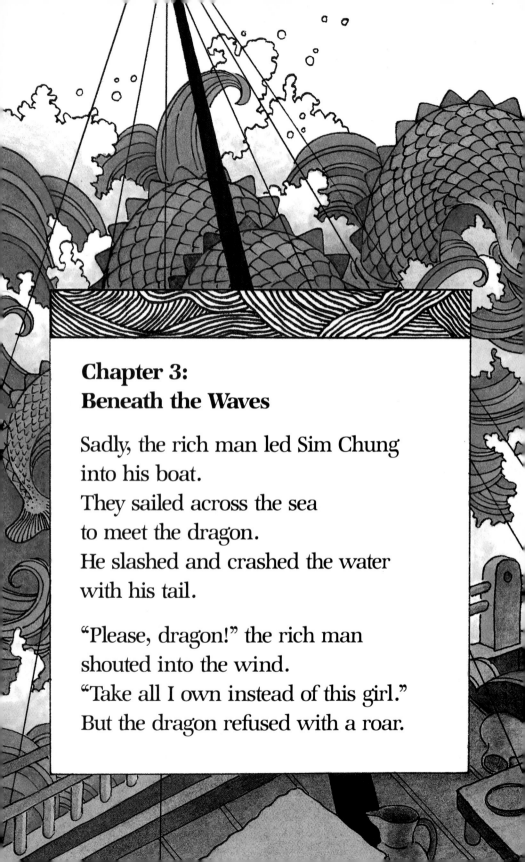

Chapter 3:
Beneath the Waves

Sadly, the rich man led Sim Chung
into his boat.
They sailed across the sea
to meet the dragon.
He slashed and crashed the water
with his tail.

"Please, dragon!" the rich man
shouted into the wind.
"Take all I own instead of this girl."
But the dragon refused with a roar.

Then Sim Chung leaped into the water.
Suddenly, the wild waves turned
smooth and calm as a mirror.
She sank swiftly beneath the water,
through gardens of plants,
past fish as bright as birds.

She floated through the gates
of a shining palace.
She bowed low
before the dragon.
Her courage melted his rage.

"Welcome, Sim Chung,"
said the dragon.
"Welcome to my watery kingdom.
I will do all I can
to make you happy."

Sea-maidens dressed Sim Chung
in fine silk robes.
They fed her the fruits of the sea.
They sang her to sleep under pearls
as big and bright as moons.

Sim Chung was grateful
for the dragon's kindness.
But thoughts of her father
were always in her heart.

The dragon knew of her sadness.
One morning he called Sim Chung.
"You have lived in my kingdom
without complaint," he told her.
"And you have shown great love
for your father.

Now it is time to return
and find him."
Sim Chung bowed before the dragon.
She said good-bye with a grateful heart.

Sea-maidens led Sim Chung to a giant lotus
on the bottom of the sea.
The blossom closed around Sim Chung,
then pushed up toward the sun.
It soon came to rest
beside the rich man's boat.

What a lovely blossom, he thought.
He took it home and
put it gently in his garden pool.
He did not know that Sim Chung
still slept in the heart of the flower.

At midnight Sim Chung woke.
She came out to drink dew from the petals.
Just at that moment, the smell
of the blossom woke the rich man.
When he saw Sim Chung in the starlight,
he knew her at once.

Love bloomed like a flower in his heart.
"Will you marry me?" he asked.
Now Sim Chung knew the rich man
was good and kind.
But still she answered,
"Not yet. First I must find my father."

Chapter 4:
The Search

Sim Chung searched everywhere
for her father.
She searched their old home.
She searched the streets.
She searched the temple.
But he was searching for her, too,
so they never met.

Finally, Sim Chung asked
the rich man for help.
"Will you give a feast and invite all
who are old and blind?" she said.
"Perhaps then I will find my father."

The rich man agreed at once.
And for three nights, many people
came to feast in his courtyard.

Sim Chung gazed through the curtains,
hoping to see her father.
On the third night,
just as the feast began,
servants started to close the gates.
They shut out a torn old man
with legs as thin as threads.

Sim Chung gave a cry of joy
and ran to the old man.
"Father! Dear Father!"
Her tears fell into his eyes.
"Sim Chung!" he cried with joy.
"If only I could see your face!"

The old man rubbed tears from his eyes.
He did not know if they were his
or Sim Chung's.
But suddenly he could see her face.

Sim Chung brought her father
to the rich man.
"Welcome, Father," the rich man said,
and bowed low.
"Now our joy will be complete."

Hand in hand, they joined the feast.
And forever after,
Sim Chung shone like a star
in both their hearts.